CATCH IT IF YOU CAN

Nursery verses compiled by
BRIAN THOMPSON
Illustrated by
SUSIE JENKIN-PEARCE

VIKING KESTREL

For Michael and Rebecca Neate of Bairnsdale,
Australia
and Rosie and Victoria Jenkin of Boston,
England.

Acknowledgements

Many people have helped in the selection of verses for this
collection, and I am very grateful for their help. I would
particularly like to acknowledge the contribution of Cathy
and Kara Veitch and Elizabeth Attenborough.
Pam and Catherine Alexander, Carole Ritchie, Heather
Avigdor and Carolyn Sayles all gave most generously of
time, taste and enthusiasm. Their responses were most
useful in making the final difficult choices. Their
sensitivity to children's responses and delight in poetry for
children are reflected in *Catch it if you can.*

Brian Thompson
London, 1989

The compiler and publishers gratefully acknowledge permission to reproduce copyright poems
in this book:

'Cats' by Eleanor Farjeon from *The Children's Bells* published by Oxford University Press,
reprinted by permission of David Higham Associates Ltd; 'The Frog on the Log' by Ilo Orleans,
reprinted by permission of Karen S. Solomon; 'Outdoor Song' by A. A. Milne from *The House at
Pooh Corner,* copyright in the U.S.A. by E. P. Dutton, renewed 1956 by A. A. Milne, reprinted by
permission of the publisher E. P. Dutton, a division of NAL Penguin Inc., Methuen Children's
Books and the Canadian Publishers, McClelland and Stewart, Toronto; 'The Song of the Train'
from *One at a Time* by David McCord, copyright 1952 by David McCord, reprinted by
permission of Little, Brown and Company; 'The Tickle Rhyme', © 1950 Ian Serraillier, from *The
Monster Horse* published by Oxford University Press; 'Toaster Time' from *There is No Rhyme for
Silver* by Eve Merriam, copyright © 1962 by Eve Merriam, all rights reserved, reprinted by kind
permission of Marian Reiner for the author; 'Understanding' from *The Moon and a Star and Other
Poems* by Myra Cohn Livingston, copyright © 1965 by Myra Cohn Livingston, reprinted by
permission of Marian Reiner for the author; 'Wasps' reprinted by permission of G. P. Putnam's
Sons from *Is Anybody Hungry?* by Dorothy Aldis, text © 1964 by Dorothy Aldis.

Every effort has been made to trace copyright holders, but in a few cases this has proved
impossible. The compiler and publishers apologize for these cases of unwilling copyright
transgression and would like to hear from any copyright holders not acknowledged.

VIKING KESTREL

Published by the Penguin Group
27 Wrights Lane, London W8 5TZ, England
Viking Penguin Inc., 40 West 23rd Street, New York, New York 10010, USA
Penguin Books Australia Ltd, Ringwood, Victoria, Australia
Penguin Books Canada Ltd, 2801 John Street, Markham, Ontario, Canada L3R 1B4
Penguin Books (NZ) Ltd, 182-190 Wairau Road, Auckland 10, New Zealand

Penguin Books Ltd, Registered Offices: Harmondsworth, Middlesex, England

First published 1989

10 9 8 7 6 5 4 3 2 1

This selection copyright © Brian Thompson, 1989
Illustrations copyright © Susie Jenkin-Pearce, 1989

Typeset in Linotron 202 Baskerville by
Rowland Phototypesetting (London) Limited
Printed in Great Britain by William Clowes Limited, Beccles and London

A CIP catalogue record for this book is available from the British Library

ISBN 0-670-82279-5

Humpty Dumpty

Humpty Dumpty sat on a wall,
Eating black bananas.
Where do you think he put the skins?
Down the king's pyjamas.

Anonymous

Something About Me

There's something about me
That I'm knowing.
There's something about me
That isn't showing.

I'm growing!

Anonymous

The Tadpole

Underneath the water-weeds,
  Small and black, I wriggle,
And life is most surprising!
  Wiggle! waggle! wiggle!
There's every now and then a most
  Exciting change in me,
I wonder, wiggle! waggle!
  What I shall turn out to be.

Elizabeth Gould

Miss Polly had a Dolly

Miss Polly had a dolly who was sick, sick, sick,
So she phoned for the doctor to be quick, quick, quick.
The doctor came with his bag and his hat,
And he knocked on the door with a rat-a-tat-tat.

He looked at the dolly and he shook his head,
And he said, "Miss Polly, put her straight to bed."
He wrote on a paper for a pill, pill, pill,
"I'll be back in the morning with my bill, bill, bill."

Anonymous

Little Arabella Miller

Little Arabella Miller
Found a woolly caterpillar.
First it crawled upon her mother,
Then upon her baby brother;
All said, "Arabella Miller,
Take away this caterpillar."

Anonymous

The Tickle Rhyme

"Who's that tickling my back?" said the wall.
"Me," said a small
Caterpillar. "I'm learning
To crawl."

Ian Serraillier

Round and Round the Garden

Round and round the garden
Like a teddy bear;
   One step,
   Two steps,
And tickle me under there!

Round and round the lighthouse
Went the spiral stair;
   One step,
   Two steps,
Right up in the air!

Round and round the haystack
Like a little mouse;
   One step,
   Two steps,
In his little house.

Anonymous

Toaster Time

Tick tick tick tick tick tick tick
Toast up a sandwich quick quick quick
Hamwich
Or jamwich
Lick lick lick!

Tick tick tick tick tick tick – stop!
  POP!

Eve Merriam

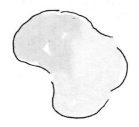

The Pancake

Mix a pancake,
Stir a pancake,
   Pop it in the pan.

Fry the pancake,
Toss the pancake,
   Catch it if you can.

Christina Rossetti

The Frog on the Log

There once
Was a green
   Little frog, frog, frog –

Who played
In the wood
   On a log, log, log!

A screech owl
Sitting
   In a tree, tree, tree –

Came after
The frog
　　With a scree, scree, scree!

When the frog
Heard the owl –
　　In a flash, flash, flash –

He leaped
In the pond
　　With a splash, splash, splash!

Ilo Orleans

I Wish I was a little Grub

I wish I was a little grub
With whiskers round my tummy,
I'd climb into a honey-pot
And make my tummy gummy.

Anonymous

Wasps

Wasps like coffee.
Syrup.
Tea.
Coca-Cola.
Butter.
Me.

Dorothy Aldis

Jelly on your Plate

Jelly on your plate,
Jelly on your plate,
Wibble, wobble,
Wibble, wobble,
Jelly on your plate.

Jelly on your spoon,
Jelly on your spoon,
Wibble, wobble,
Wibble, wobble,
Jelly on your spoon.

Jelly in your tum,
Jelly in your tum,
Wibble, wobble,
Wibble, wobble,
Jelly in your tum.

Anonymous

Algy Met a Bear

Algy met a bear;
The bear met Algy.
The bear grew bulgy;
The bulge was Algy.

Anonymous

Fuzzy Wuzzy was a Bear

Fuzzy Wuzzy was a bear;
Fuzzy Wuzzy had no hair.
So Fuzzy Wuzzy wasn't fuzzy,
Was he?

Anonymous

Understanding

Sun
and rain
and wind
and storms
and thunder go together.

There has to be a little bit of each to make the weather.

Myra Cohn Livingston

Outdoor Song

The more it
SNOWS – tiddely-pom
The more it
GOES – tiddely-pom
The more it
GOES – tiddely-pom
On
Snowing.

And nobody
KNOWS – tiddely-pom
How cold my
TOES – tiddely-pom
How cold my
TOES – tiddely-pom
Are
Growing.

A. A. Milne

Tiny Tim

I have a little brother
His name is Tiny Tim,
I put him in the bathtub
To teach him how to swim.
He drank up all the water;
He ate up all the soap;
He lay down on the bathmat
Blowing bubbles from his throat.

In came the doctor,
In came the nurse,
In came the lady
With the alligator purse.
"Naughty!" said the doctor.
"Wicked!" said the nurse.
"Wind," said the lady
With the alligator purse.

Anonymous

Song of the Train

Clickety-clack,
Wheels on the track,
This is the way
They begin the attack:
Click-ety-clack,
Click-ety-clack,
Click-ety, *clack*-ety,
Click-ety
Clack.

Clickety-clack,
Over the crack,
Faster and faster
The song of the track:
Clickety-clack,
Clickety-clack,
Clickety, clackety,
Clackety
Clack.

Riding in front,
Riding in back,
Everyone hears
The song of the track:
Clickety-clack,
Clickety-clack,
Clickety, *clickety,*
Clackety
Clack.

David McCord

Cats

Cats sleep
Anywhere,
Any table,
Any chair,
Top of piano,
Window ledge,
In the middle,
On the edge,
Open drawer,
Empty shoe,
Anybody's
Lap will do,
Fitted in a
Cardboard box,
In the cupboard
With your frocks –
Anywhere!
They don't care!
Cats sleep
Anywhere.

Eleanor Farjeon

Five Little Peas

Five little peas in a pea-pod pressed,
One grew, two grew and so did all the rest.
They grew and they grew and they did not stop,
Till all of a sudden the pod went POP.

Anonymous

Little Piggy-wig

Little piggy-wig on the farm close by,
All by himself ran away from the sty.
The dog said "Woof",
The cow said "Moo",
The sheep said "Baa",
The dove said "Coo".
Little piggy-wig began to cry,
And as fast as he could he ran back to the sty.

Anonymous

Christmas is Coming

Christmas is coming
   And the geese are getting fat,
Please to put a penny
   In the old man's hat;
If you haven't got a penny,
   A ha'penny will do.
If you haven't got a ha'penny,
   God bless you!

Anonymous